A PREDICTABLE WORD BOOK

THE TRICKY TWINS

Story by Janie Spaht Gill, Ph.D.
Illustrations by Bob Reese

ARO PUBLISHING

The twins Paul and Pat look exactly the same.

The only thing not alike
was they had different names.

On the first day of school
they dressed exactly the same.

"Oh dear," said the teacher.
"How will I learn their names?"

When the two turned around, each child's name showed on the back.

"Great," said the teacher. "You are Paul and you are Pat."

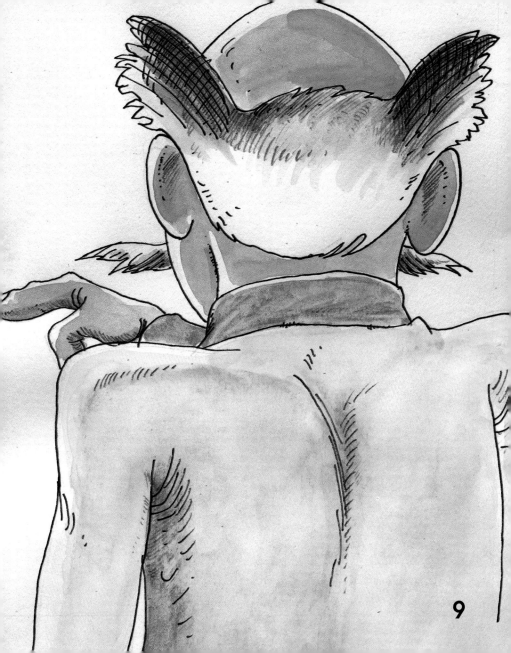

9

On the second day of school their shirts were the same.

"Oh dear," said the teacher. "How will I learn their names?"

11

But their haircuts were different
when they took off their hats.

"Great," said the teacher.
"You are Paul and you are Pat."

3

On the third day of school their haircuts were the same.

"Oh dear," said the teacher. "How will I learn their names?"

But their names were written on their socks, one in orange and one in black.

"Great," said the teacher. "You are Paul and you are Pat."

17

On the fourth day of school their socks looked the same.

"Oh dear," said the teacher. "How will I learn their names?"

But when the children grinned,
the teacher happily exclaimed.

"Now you can not trick me, because
I have learned your names.

There's something that you can not change that I see after all.

One of you has lost a tooth and that one of you is Paul."

But when the teacher looked again,
their smiles were just the same.

The teacher cried, "Oh, dear me.
I have been tricked again!"

23